SAMMY SPIDER'S
FIRST
BAR MITZVAH

This
PJ BOOK
belongs to

_____

_____

PJ Library®

JEWISH BEDTIME STORIES and SONGS

I look forward to celebrating the bar & bat mitzvahs of my grandchildren Hayden, Derek, Leo and Eden —S.A.R.

To Arielle, Lila and Jonah, Sammy's very good friends in New York. Keep visiting us!—K.J.K.

Text copyright © 2016 by Sylvia A. Rouss
Illustrations copyright © 2016 by Katherine Janus Kahn

KAR-BEN PUBLISHING
A division of Lerner Publishing Group, Inc.
241 First Avenue North
Minneapolis, MN 55401 USA
1-800-4-KARBEN

Website address: www.karben.com

Library of Congress Cataloging-in-Publication Data

Names: Rouss, Sylvia A., author. | Kahn, Katherine, illustrator.
Title: Sammy Spider's first Bar Mitzvah / by Sylvia A. Rouss ;
    illustrated by Katherine Janus Kahn.
Description: Minneapolis : Kar-Ben Publishing, [2016] | Summary:
    Josh's cousin Ben is having his bar mitzvah, and Sammy ends
    up coming along! He gets a view of the Torah readings, the
    blessings . . . and one tradition that gets this silly little spider
    into even more trouble than usual.
Identifiers: LCCN 2015040982 (print) | LCCN 2016004620 (ebook) |
    ISBN 9781467789318 (lb : alk. paper) | ISBN 9781467794121 (pb
    : alk. paper) | ISBN 9781512409406 (eb pdf)
Subjects: | CYAC: Bar-mitzvah—Fiction. | Spiders—Fiction.
Classification: LCC PZ7.R7622 Sac 2016 (print) | LCC PZ7.R7622
    (ebook) | DDC [E]—dc23

LC record available at http://lccn.loc.gov/2015040982

PJ Library Edition ISBN 978-1-5415-4645-5

Manufactured in Hong Kong
1-45641-41654-3/29/2018

101828.1K1/B1281/A4

SAMMY SPIDER'S
FIRST
BAR MITZVAH

Sylvia A. Rouss

Illustrated by
Katherine Janus Kahn

KAR-BEN
PUBLISHING

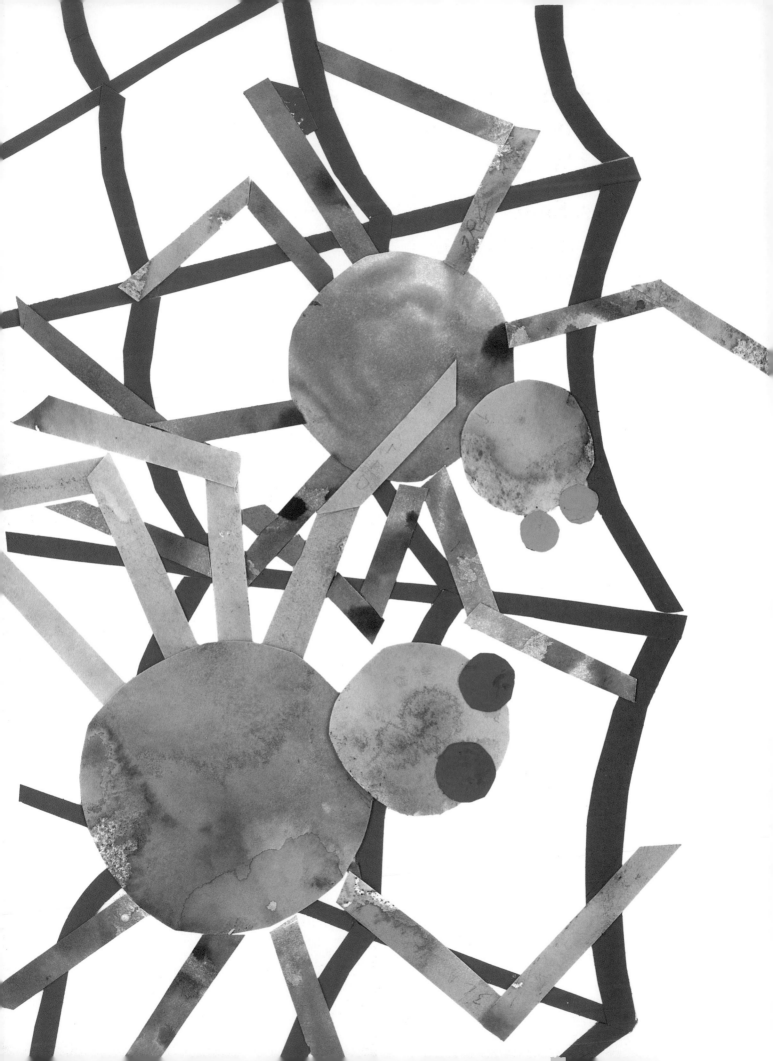

Sammy Spider looked down from his web at the zippered velvet bag lying on the table. "Mother!" he yelled. "What is that?"

"That's Mr. Shapiro's tallit bag, where he keeps his tallit and his kippah," said Mrs. Spider.

"Josh's cousin Ben is celebrating his bar mitzvah today, and the Shapiros are going to the synagogue. Ben is thirteen, so he is old enough to help lead the Shabbat service and read from the Torah."

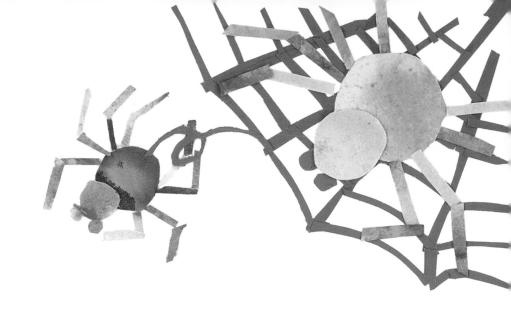

"Am I old enough to celebrate a bar mitzvah, too?" asked Sammy.

"Silly little Sammy," laughed Mrs. Spider. "Spiders don't celebrate bar mitzvahs. Spiders spin webs."

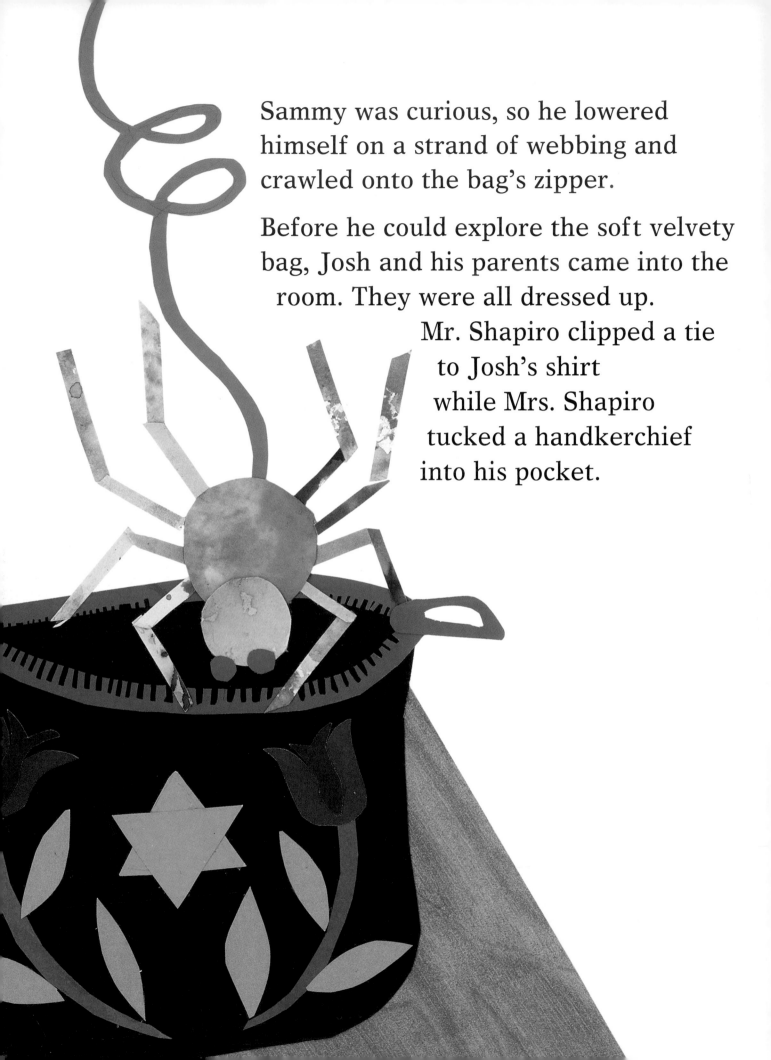

Sammy was curious, so he lowered himself on a strand of webbing and crawled onto the bag's zipper.

Before he could explore the soft velvety bag, Josh and his parents came into the room. They were all dressed up. Mr. Shapiro clipped a tie to Josh's shirt while Mrs. Shapiro tucked a handkerchief into his pocket.

"I'll carry the tallit bag!" Josh announced. He picked up the bag—with Sammy still clinging to it.

"Bye, Mother," whispered Sammy excitedly. "I guess I'm going to Ben's bar mitzvah."

Sammy clung to the tallit bag all the way to the synagogue. Then Josh put the tallit bag down on the shelf of prayer books in the front hall, and Sammy scurried off.

Sammy noticed a bowl of candy on the table and scurried over to take a closer look. He climbed into the bowl. The candy was wrapped in stiff colorful paper.

Just then Sammy saw Mr. Shapiro's hand appear above him. Mr. Shapiro picked up a handful of candy—and one tiny spider. Sammy held onto the candy tightly as Mr. Shapiro slipped him into his jacket pocket along with the candy.

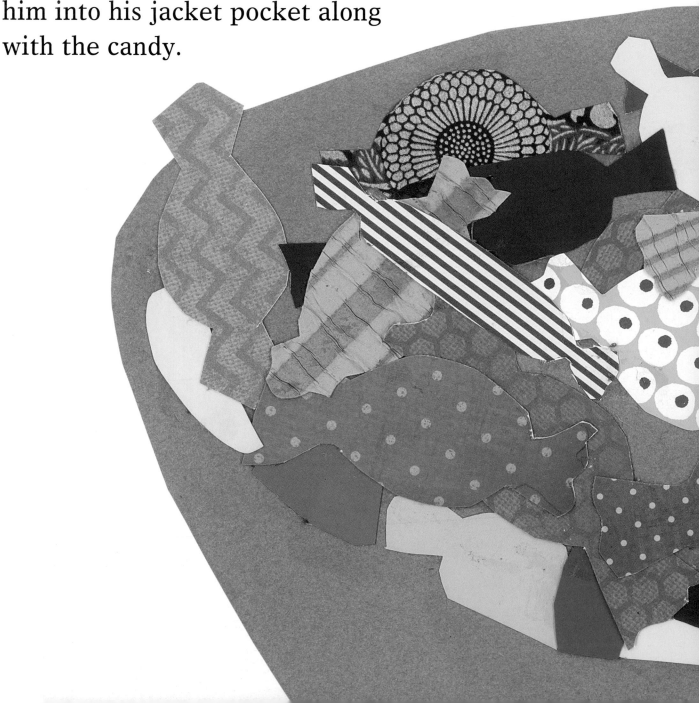

"Oh no!" thought Sammy.
"What will happen to me now?"

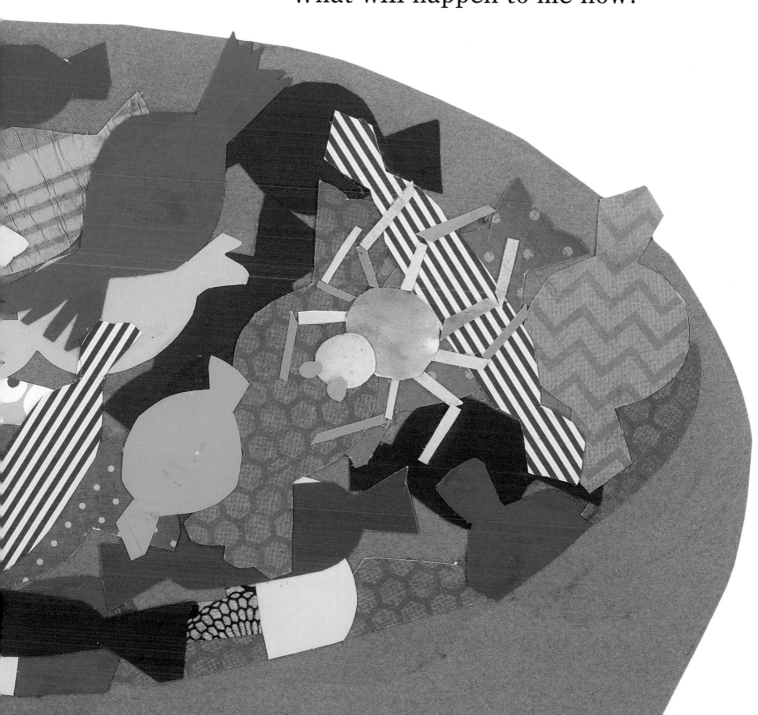

Sammy peeked out from Mr. Shapiro's
pocket. He saw Ben and his family
standing on the bimah with the rabbi
and the cantor. Ben's parents draped a
beautiful tallit across Ben's shoulders.

The service began. The Ark was opened, and Sammy saw the Torahs inside.

"They're beautiful!" thought Sammy.

He watched the rabbi remove a Torah from the Ark and give it to Ben, who carried it around the synagogue while he sang a beautiful prayer.

As Ben walked past Josh and his parents, they gently touched the Torah's soft velvety cover with their prayer books. Then Sammy watched Ben return to the bimah, where the rabbi carefully unrolled the Torah.

Sammy settled down with the candies in Mr. Shapiro's pocket and listened to Ben singing in Hebrew and reading from the Torah.

Sammy thought, "I wish I knew how to read from the Torah. What a special thing to do!" But he remembered that spiders don't celebrate bar mitzvahs. Spiders spin webs.

Ben finished reading and beamed happily.
Everyone in the synagogue shouted, "Mazel Tov!"

"May you have a sweet life filled with Torah and
good deeds," said the rabbi.

Suddenly the air was filled
with flying candies as
people in the synagogue
tossed candies toward
the bar mitzvah boy. Mr.
Shapiro reached into
his pocket for his candy,
too, and tossed it at Ben.
Sammy, still clutching one
of the pieces, went flying
through the air and landed
near the bimah.

A shower of
sweets dropped
all around him.

Then Sammy heard little running feet, as happy children dashed to the bimah to gather the treats.

Sammy wrapped his legs tightly around his piece of candy.

Luckily it was Josh who picked up the piece of candy to which Sammy was clinging and put it into his pocket. Sammy breathed a sigh of relief.

When the Shapiros arrived home, Sammy sneaked out of Josh's pocket and climbed up to his web.

"I'm glad to be back!" he said as he snuggled with his mother. "How was the bar mitzvah?" asked Mrs. Spider.

"It was a very special day for Ben," said Sammy. "I hope he has a sweet life filled with Torah, like the rabbi said. And I hope *I* have a sweet life full of spinning webs!"

About the Bar/Bat Mitzvah: A bar mitzvah (for a boy) or bat mitzvah (for a girl) is the Jewish coming-of-age celebration. When a Jewish child reaches the age of 13, he or she is regarded as ready to have the responsibilities of a Jewish adult in terms of religious observance. The bar or bat mitzvah is celebrated by the child being called to read from the Torah for the first time. As in this story, in many congregations, the congregants and guests throw candies toward the child to wish him or her a sweet life filled with Torah and good deeds.

Sylvia A. Rouss is an award-winning author and early childhood educator, the creator of the popular Sammy Spider series which celebrated its 20th anniversary in 2013 with over 800,000 Sammy Spider books sold. She lives in Tarzana, California.

Katherine Janus Kahn, an illustrator, calligrapher, and sculptor, studied Fine Arts at the Bezalel School in Jerusalem and at the University of Iowa. She has illustrated many children's books including Kar-Ben's popular Sammy Spider series and many other award-winning books for young children. She lives in Wheaton, Maryland.